EMILY ARNOLD McCULLY

Popcorn at the Palace

BROWNDEER PRESS   HARCOURT BRACE & COMPANY

San Diego   New York   London

Browndeer Press is a registered trademark of Harcourt Brace & Company.

Library of Congress Cataloging-in-Publication Data
McCully, Emily Arnold.
Popcorn at the palace/Emily Arnold McCully.
p.   cm.
"Browndeer Press."
Summary: In the mid-1800's Maisie Ferris and her father travel
to England to introduce the American phenomenon of popcorn.
ISBN 0-15-277699-0
[1. Popcorn—Fiction.   2. Fathers and daughters—Fiction.
3. England—Fiction.]   I. Title.
PZ7M478415Po   1997
[E]—dc20   96-17592

First edition   F E D C B A

Printed in Singapore

To Sam and Ida Griesemer

In 1837, a devout and enterprising band of pioneers led by the Reverend George Washington Gale founded Galesburg in Illinois. Galesburgers protected themselves from sin on the wild frontier. They lived according to the Scriptures and frowned on anything too different. All except Olmsted Ferris...

MAISIE FERRIS took after her open-minded father. Most families in Galesburg had only the Bible in their new parlors, but Olmsted and his wife, Concurrance Ann Ferris, kept up with the latest books and even a few magazines, such as *Knickerbocker* and *Godey's*. Their stories about the English royal family intrigued Maisie the most.

Reading about things that were different excited Maisie's imagination. The endless, flat, fertile prairie, ablaze with flowers, excited her father's. He decided to try growing mustard. While it grew, he invented a machine for threshing it.

Then he thought he'd try planting canary seed, figuring it could be threshed with the same machine. The Ferrises' neighbors raised ordinary corn and hogs.

Olmsted's ideas shocked them.

As it turned out, no one wanted to buy mustard or canary seed, but this didn't discourage Olmsted. While he kept thinking and tinkering, Maisie made herself a dollhouse out of wood scraps, and doll furniture out of bits of leather. Then she made a doll from a corn husk and named it Victoria.

At church, people were stiff with Olmsted and Concurrance Ann. "Why don't they plant corn and raise hogs, the way they're supposed to?" they asked one another. Their children were standoffish with Maisie. "What's that dolly called?" one girl asked.

"Victoria," Maisie said.

"What kind of name is that?"

"It's the name of the Queen of England," Maisie replied. "She got married a while back."

"The Queen of England? Ain't you an American? We don't hold with royalty here! Maisie Ferris, you ought to be ashamed!"

"I just liked the sound," Maisie said.

One day, a journalist from England came to town to report on how the pioneers were faring. Maisie overheard him ask why a small field of corn looked different from the rest.

She spoke up. "Why, that's popcorn!"

"Popcorn?"

"It grows on ears, like other corn. You dry the kernels. In a pot over a hot fire, they puff up and turn white."

The Englishman said that such a thing was unheard-of where he'd come from. Maisie ran to find her father.

"Papa! In England, they've never heard of popcorn! I bet you they'd take to it just as we do, if only they knew!" Olmsted put on a considering look.

That night, he announced that he was going to take popcorn to England, along with some cattle.

It was just the enterprise he'd been looking for. There might be a huge market overseas. He would show the English just how spectacular American prairie products could be!

Next spring, Olmsted planted sixty of his best acres in popcorn. The good people of Galesburg could hardly bring themselves to speak civilly to him. It was all out of proportion! Popcorn wasn't real food. And the English had never heard of it. Why would they buy any?

The popcorn kernels filled twenty barrels, even more than Olmsted expected. "It's Illinois!" he crowed. "It's this rich prairie that grows everything bigger and better!"

"Papa, I want to go with you," Maisie said.

"It's a business trip, dearie," Olmsted replied. "What would I do with you?"

"I want to see the Queen," Maisie said.

"The Queen of England doesn't take time for folks like us, Maisie," said Olmsted, laughing.

"It was my idea, Papa. And I could be a help to you," Maisie said.

Her mother agreed.

Olmsted relented. Galesburgers were convinced the devil had gotten into him. He and Maisie took stagecoaches and canal boats to New York and from there sailed for Dover.

The trip lasted three weeks. Maisie passed the time discussing books with another interesting Englishman who had just toured America, the author Charles Dickens.

In London, Olmsted had no trouble selling his cattle, but when he mentioned popcorn, he got blank looks. "They don't know the excellence of our American product," he said to Maisie.

Maisie kept quiet for the first few days. Then she said, "Papa, it's time to see the Queen!"

"Maisie, you know we can't do that," her father said.

"Take me to the palace, please," Maisie begged.

Olmsted sighed and took her to Buckingham Palace. They watched the changing of the guard. Maisie wanted to wait to see the Queen. A policeman told them the Queen was out of town. Olmsted tried to comfort Maisie, but he had popcorn on his mind.

Finally, the manager of an entertainment parlor on Regent Street agreed to let Olmsted do a public demonstration of popcorn. Posters were put up and a small crowd gathered.

Olmsted showed a handful of dried-up little popcorn kernels. A fire was lighted and Maisie tossed the kernels into a pot.

The results were amazing. "It's corn that turns to snow!" someone cried. Served up with butter and salt, popcorn delighted the crowd even more.

Olmsted and Maisie had to repeat their performance many times. Word of the exploding food spread all over London. This cheered Maisie up, but she wouldn't let go of her wish. When was the Queen coming home?

As Olmsted and Maisie rested in their room, there was a knock on the door. The hotel manager was very agitated. "I am to request a private showing, sir," he said. "His Majesty the Prince Consort has heard of your popcorn and wishes to see it. You are to be presented to the Palace three days hence."

"Whoopee!" shouted Olmsted. "A man after my own heart!"

Maisie was pale. "The Prince!" she whispered. "Prince Albert! He's Queen Victoria's husband!"

The hotel manager reappeared. "Mr. Ferris. Sir. There is an etiquette to being presented at Court. A lady-in-waiting to the Queen is here to teach it to you."

"Shucks," said Olmsted.

The lady-in-waiting coached Maisie and Olmsted for the next two days on how to approach royalty, how to bow, how to speak when spoken to, and what to say. They were never to ask a direct question of the royal couple, or to turn their backs to them. Maisie curtsied over and over, until her head swam.

The great day arrived. A carriage came and drove them to Windsor.

Maisie and her father waited. Soon, a page announced
that the Queen and her Consort would receive them. Maisie's
heart flipped.

When the door was flung open, Olmsted, in his eagerness,
forgot what he had practiced.

He shot toward the royal couple, smiling broadly. "Howdy-do," he roared, but fortunately he stopped short of shaking hands. Queen Victoria looked alarmed, but the Prince Consort managed a smile. "Pleased to meet you," Olmsted went on. "This is my girl Maisie." Maisie blushed crimson.

Olmsted showed his kernels, and Maisie dropped them into a hot pot provided by a footman. The popping corn battered the lid. The Queen clapped like a child. After the first batch, she and Albert asked to see the corn turn to snow again.

"This is peculiarly American," Prince Albert observed.

"Right you are!" said Olmsted. "Greatest nation on earth!"

"How might we grow it here?" asked Albert politely.

"You could send for a few acres of Illinois soil!" said Olmsted.

"Ahem," said Prince Albert.

The Queen said she would like to present Olmsted with a gift.

"Oh, I can't accept any gift," he said. So the Queen beckoned to Maisie, who was drinking in the sight of royalty. "What is that you are holding?" the Queen asked.

"My doll, mum," said Maisie.

"And what is she called?" asked the Queen.

"Victoria, mum," said Maisie.

"Indeed," the Queen said. "I will give you something to take home."

The lady-in-waiting handed Maisie a French wax doll with real hair and a velvet-and-lace gown. Maisie gasped. It was more beautiful by far than any she'd seen in *Godey's* or *Knickerbocker*. Such a doll was unknown on the prairie.

"Oh, thank you, mum," she said. "This is my dream come true—and more!"

The visit concluded with the Prince's order for several barrels of popcorn *and* some Illinois soil.

Maisie took the doll home to Galesburg. It was a sensation. Now everyone wanted to hear about the Queen. Other people followed Olmsted's example and dreamed up new enterprises. They couldn't stand in the way of progress, could they?

*Maisie treasured Victoria II all her life, as did her children
and theirs. Popcorn became a favorite snack of millions,
but it never caught on in England.*

AUTHOR'S NOTE

Galesburg, Illinois, is my hometown.

Gale and his associates had already planned the town, and Knox, the college at its center, before they arrived. Among the families committed to the noble experiment were the many Ferrises. The Olmsted in my story is pretty much as Ernest Elmo Calkins describes him in the 1937 history, *They Broke the Prairie* (Charles Scribner's Sons, New York): "Always on the lookout for novelties . . . the most adventurous of Silvanus' sons." He and Concurrance Ann arrived in Illinois with a cupful of timothy seed. They imported the first sheep, set up a sawmill, and grew the popcorn that Olmsted took to London.

I have invented a daughter named Maisie, but Olmsted had one, her name lost to us now. The Queen gave Olmsted a doll to take home for her, and the doll was passed on through generations, according to Calkins, until it fell apart.

Galesburg prospered and became a major railroad hub. I remember listening as a child for the sound of the Zephyr on its way to California. Carl Sandburg was born in Galesburg, and Knox College has produced many distinguished citizens.

E. A. M.